Crum

Story of the American Revolution Coloring Book

BY PETER COPELAND

DOVER PUBLICATIONS, INC., NEW YORK

Introduction

The American Revolution was a war of independence or separation, in which the British colonies severed their connection with the Crown, but kept their society much as it had been before the war.

A long series of acts passed by Parliament made the Colonies break with the motherland: the Writs of Assistance (1761), the Proclamation of 1763, the Stamp Act (1765), the Townshend Acts (1767), the Tea Act (1773) and the Intolerable Acts (1774). These and other actions by the Crown threatened both the prosperity of the colonies and what the colonists had come to regard as their rights according to the (unwritten) British constitution.

The colonists had meetings that led to the First Continental Congress (1774) and the Second Continental Congress (1775-76), which eventually established the goal of separation from Britain. Discussions of a peaceful solution ceased and war began.

Although the colonists had little experience in the military arts, they put great faith in the ability of untrained citizen-soldiers to fight for the preservation of their liberties. Under the leadership of George Washington and a few former colonial and foreign officers, an army was formed which, through the course of many heartbreaking defeats and constant hunger and hardship, would keep the professional armies of Great Britain at bay until, with French and other foreign assistance, they were able to defeat the mighty British Empire after many long years of war.

The war was fought in a series of land campaigns, in which the colonists participated, either as members of the Continental Army or as members of the various state militias, and on the sea, where the French alliance was vital in intimidating British sea power.

There were Americans for whom the end of the war brought misery. The colonists whose loyalty lay with the King knew only bitterness and defeat, and those other, native, Americans—the Indians—gained nothing from the victory and were evicted from their ancestral lands.

At the end of the long struggle, the veterans of the Continental Army disbanded and made their way home as best they could, unpaid and unprovided for by the new government they had brought into being.

To Sean Michael Casey

Story of the American Revolution Coloring Book is a new work, first published by Dover Publications, Inc., in 1988.

DOVER *Pictorial Archive* SERIES

This book belongs to the Dover Pictorial Archive Series. You may use the designs and illustrations for graphics and crafts applications, free and without special permission, provided that you include no more than four in the same publication or project. (For permission for additional use, please write to Dover Publications, Inc., 31 East 2nd Street, Mineola, N.Y. 11501.)

However, republication or reproduction of any illustration by any other graphic service whether it be in a book or in any other design resource is strictly prohibited.

International Standard Book Number 0-486-25648-0

Manufactured in the United States of America
Dover Publications, Inc., 31 East 2nd Street, Mineola, N.Y. 11501

The Boston Massacre. The Townshend Acts passed by Parliament in 1767 placed unwelcome financial restrictions on the colonists, creating great ill-will. On March 5, 1770, an unruly, hostile mob confronted a squad of British soldiers stationed in Boston. The soldiers fired into the crowd, killing five Bostonians and wounding others.

The Boston Tea Party. Relations with England deteriorated. On the night of December 16, 1773, a band of Bostonians, angered by the British tax on tea, disguised themselves as Indians and raided three tea-laden ships in Boston harbor, dumping 342 cases of tea into the water. The English retaliated with the harsh Intolerable Acts.

Paul Revere's Ride. On the night of April 18, 1775, Boston silversmith Paul Revere galloped from Boston to Lexington to warn the colonists that British troops were advancing on Lexington and Concord to seize patriot leaders and capture the main patriot arsenal of hidden weapons. 3

The Battle of Lexington. The next morning, April 19, 1775, British soldiers reached Lexington and were confronted with two companies of patriot militiamen drawn up on the village green. Someone fired a shot and the redcoats poured several volleys into the American ranks. The militiamen fled for cover, leaving eight Massachusetts citizen-soldiers dead. This incident marked the beginning of the war.

4

The Capture of Fort Ticonderoga. The capture of this British fort on Lake Champlain, New York, on May 10, 1775, by Ethan Allen and his Green Mountain Boys gave the Americans a surprising and much-needed victory. The British commander, roused from his bed, surrendered the fort while still dressed in his nightshirt.

George Washington Appointed Commander in Chief. On July 3, 1775, George Washington of Virginia was chosen by the Continental Congress to command the American military forces assembled at Cambridge, Massachusetts. His first task was to instruct and outfit the untrained militiamen he now commanded and to try to make them into a disciplined army.

Continental Artillery

A Light Dragoon

Continental Infantry

FRIEDRICH VON STEUBEN

A Rifleman

1776

The Continental Soldier. The rustic volunteers of 1775 were more a mob than an army. George Washington drafted a plan to create 26 regiments of infantry, one regiment of riflemen and one regiment of artillery, but recruiting became, and remained, a problem. Throughout the war, most campaigns were fought using Continental Army units alongside local militia regiments. Discipline and military instruction were supplied to recruits by a former Prussian officer, Friedrich von Steuben. Through the efforts of this hardened drillmaster, the Continental soldier became a first-class fighting man.

The Battle of Bunker Hill. On the morning of June 17, 1775, British troops assaulted the positions of the American army, entrenched upon Breed's Hill outside Boston. A bloody fight developed that became known as the battle of Bunker Hill (where some of the action did take place). The King's troops, with leveled bayonets, finally put the patriot forces to flight but, as a result of the battle, the British were eventually forced to evacuate Boston and make New York City the center of their operations.

Sam Adams

Thomas Jefferson

Benjamin Franklin

Richard Henry Lee

John Adams

Robert Morris

The Patriots. The leaders of the American cause in the Revolution became convinced that the bonds between England and America must be completely severed, even though the American people were largely divided on the question of independence. Benjamin Franklin summed up the seriousness of the patriots' decision when he said, "We must all hang together, or assuredly we shall all hang separately."

9

The March to Quebec. The American expedition against Quebec, late in 1775, led by Benedict Arnold, was an attempt to induce the Canadians to join the patriot cause. The American assault on Quebec failed to take the city, and the Canadians remained loyal to the Crown.

The Attack on Charleston. The war was also waged in the South. In June 1776, a British invasion force attacked Charleston, South Carolina. In the battle that followed, the British were beaten off, and a South Carolina soldier, Sergeant William Jasper, to the cheers of his comrades, climbed the parapet of the fort to replace the flag of South Carolina, which had been shot away.

Signing the Declaration of Independence. On July 2, 1776, the Continental Congress passed a resolution calling for the independence of the 13 united colonies. On July 4, the Declaration of Independence, most of which had been written by Thomas Jefferson, was adopted. Standing in front of the table is the drafting committee (left to right): John Adams, Roger Sherman, Robert Livingston, Thomas Jefferson and Benjamin Franklin.

Glover's Regiment at the Battle of Long Island. Late in June 1776, a large British invasion force landed on Staten Island, bent on occupying New York City, which was predominantly Loyalist. In a series of battles from August to November in Brooklyn, Long Island, Manhattan, Harlem and White Plains, the British smashed American resistance and captured the city. Colonel John Glover's 14th Continental Regiment of Massachusetts, composed largely of former sailors and fishermen, manned the boats that evacuated Washington's battered forces from Long Island on the night of August 29, 1776. If General Sir William Howe, head of the British forces, had taken full advantage of his victories, the Revolution might have ended then and there.

The Execution of Nathan Hale. On September 21, 1776, Nathan Hale, an officer of the 7th Connecticut Regiment, was captured while acting as a spy behind the British lines on Long Island. He was condemned and hanged the next morning. His last words are said to have been, "I only regret that I have but one life to lose for my country."

George Washington at the Delaware. After his withdrawal from New York, Washington led his badly shaken army into New Jersey. When Howe put his army up into winter quarters, Washington struck a brilliant blow against the British. On Christmas Night, 1776, with an army of 2400 men, he crossed the Delaware River, won a great victory over the Hessian garrison at Trenton and captured the city. It was a victory that provided the patriot cause with a badly needed tonic.

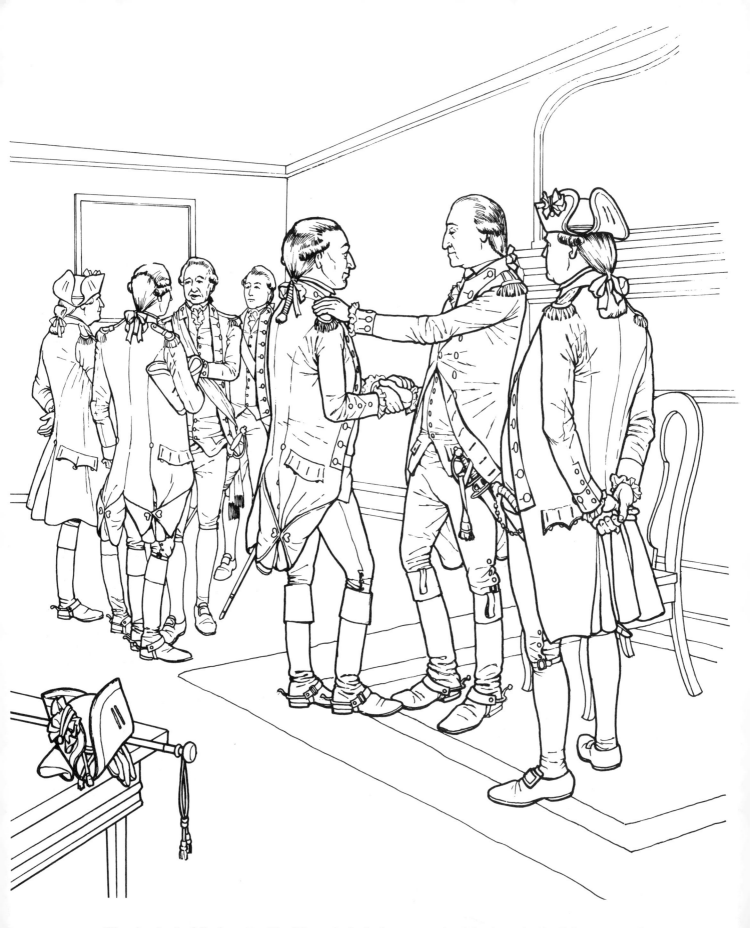

The Arrival of Lafayette. The Marquis de Lafayette arrived in America in July 1777, and volunteered his services to Congress, offering to serve without pay in the Continental Army. Lafayette met George Washington when he joined his staff of officers, and Washington realized that this young French nobleman would be most valuable in helping to bring French assistance to the patriots' cause.

The Battle of Bennington. On August 16, 1777, General John Stark led the New Hampshire militia at the Battle of Bennington in Vermont, where he defeated the German troops of General John Burgoyne in a disastrous blow to the British forces in the northern colonies.

19

The Battle of the Brandywine. In his campaign to capture Philadelphia, then the capital of the
united colonies, General Howe came close to destroying the Continental Army at Brandywine
Creek, Pennsylvania, on September 11, 1777. The patriots barely managed to escape intact, and
Lafayette was wounded.

A Loyalist Rifleman

A Highland Scottish Officer

Royal Artillery

Light Infantry

Light Dragoon

A Grenadier Officer

The British Soldier. The King's army was a well-organized, highly disciplined organization which in 1763 had defeated the French and conquered Canada at the close of the Seven Years' War. The British soldier was well trained, equipped and armed. The companies of Grenadiers and Light Infantry, the Highland Scottish, Light Dragoon, and Royal Artillery regiments were among the finest soldiers in the world. Regular British regiments were augmented with German mercenary soldiers (Hessians) and American Loyalist units.

Saratoga. Despite his defeat at Bennington, General Burgoyne pursued his campaign, but after the American victories at Freeman's Farm and Bemis Heights, his army was surrounded and forced to surrender at Saratoga, New York, on October 17, 1777. This was perhaps the most significant American victory of the entire war, for it was substantial enough to encourage France to enter into an alliance with the Americans, leading to the final victory.

Betsy Ross and the Stars and Stripes. There is a legend that Betsy Ross, who ran a shop on Arch Street in Philadelphia, was commissioned by George Washington himself to make the first American national flag. In fact, Congress adopted the Stars and Stripes on June 14, 1777 and there is no historical proof to support the legend of Betsy Ross as creator of the first national flag.

The March to Valley Forge. On December 19, 1777, the ragged, hungry soldiers of the Continental Army marched through freezing rain and snow into Valley Forge, Pennsylvania, to build winter quarters. While the British were in comfortable occupation of Philadelphia, American soldiers starved and shivered through an unusually severe winter in the barren hills, without adequate blankets, clothing or food supplies. Despite their suffering, the American troops underwent von Steuben's program of training and discipline which left the army, by spring, a more professional and efficient force than it had ever been.

Hesse-Cassel
Artillery

Hessian Grenadier
Officer

Brunswick
Dragoon

German Mercenary Troops. During the war years, about 17,000 German soldiers, most of them Hessians, were hired by the British to fight in America. They were well-trained, disciplined soldiers, clad in colorful uniforms. They did good service for their employers. Many deserted at the end of the war to settle in the newly independent United States.

The Battle of Monmouth. The Continental Army left Valley Forge in the spring of 1778 to attack the British army in New Jersey while it was on the march from Philadelphia to New York. (Howe had become nervous about his position in Philadelphia when France entered the war.) General Charles Lee commanded the American attack with such incompetence that what

should have been an American victory became a bloody drawn battle, the last major one waged in the North. It was here that "Molly Pitcher" (Mary Ludwig Hays McCauley) took over a gunner's position that had been manned by her husband, who had fainted in the heat. She served the cannon throughout the fight, becoming a legend in the Continental Army.

The Wyoming Massacre. On July 3, 1778, a force of Loyalist troops and Iroquois Indians attacked the fort at Wyoming on the Pennsylvania frontier, massacred the defenders of the fort and scalped the survivors. The Indian allies of the British fought their own style of brutal warfare, encouraged by the Loyalists, who had themselves suffered and been driven from their homes by the patriot forces.

Cherokee Brave

Iroquois Brave

War Clubs

The Indians. The British, with outposts and forts on the Great Lakes and along the Canadian frontier, were able to recruit various Indian tribes as allies in their war against the colonists. The Fox, Chippewa, Ottawa and Miami tribesmen raided frontier settlements in Kentucky. The tribes of the Six Nations, allied with the Loyalists, raided along the Pennsylvania and New York frontiers until the end of the war.

The Arrival of the French Fleet. In July 1778, the alliance with France brought a strong French fleet under Admiral d'Estaing to the shores of America, convoying transport ships loaded with supplies for the hard-pressed Continental Army. Now British naval command of American waters was no longer undisputed.

The Fall of Vincennes. In February 1779, George Rogers Clark, a young Virginian, with a force of less than 200 men, made a long and cruel wilderness march through flooded prairies and forests to capture the fortified British post at Vincennes, in what is now Indiana. The frontier of British power in the Old Northwest Indian country was, by this action, driven back to the region of Detroit.

The Battle of Flamborough Head. The combined action of naval vessels and privateers brought the war to Britain itself. A fierce sea battle was fought off the English coast on September 23, 1779, when John Paul Jones, commanding the American 40-gun man-of-war *Bonhomme Richard*, attacked a British convoy and engaged the 50-gun British man-of-war

32

Serapis. "I have not yet begun to fight!" cried Jones when called upon to surrender his battered ship. It was *Serapis* that finally surrendered, while on fire, and one of the few American naval victories of the war was achieved.

Stony Point. Minor action continued in the North after Monmouth. George Washington sent Anthony Wayne with 1300 light infantrymen to attack the British fort at Stony Point on the Hudson, 35 miles north of New York City. On the night of July 15, 1779, the Americans stormed and captured the fort at bayonet point. The fort was then dismantled.

The Capture of Major André. American General Benedict Arnold betrayed his country by attempting to deliver up the American fort at West Point to the British, using Major John André as his British contact in the plot. André was captured in disguise behind the American lines by two alert sentries as he was heading toward the British lines. Major André was tried by an American court martial as a spy and was executed on October 2, 1780.

The Battle of Camden. Although the war had slowed in the North, in the South it raged unabated. A disaster befell the American cause at Camden, South Carolina, on August 15, 1780, when an American army led by General Horatio Gates was cut to pieces and fled from the field, leaving the British under Lord Cornwallis in control of the Southern states, opposed only by scattered guerilla bands.

The Battle of Cowpens. The Americans finally began to win clear-cut victories in the South. In October 1780, a British army was decimated at Kings Mountain, South Carolina, and, early in 1781, General Daniel Morgan trapped a British army at Cowpens, South Carolina, and won a striking victory, most of the redcoat force being killed or captured.

Guilford Courthouse. Cornwallis found victory in the South elusive. At the close of the fierce battle of Guilford Courthouse, North Carolina, fought on March 15, 1781, the Americans, under General Nathaniel Greene, retreated. But the battle had left the British so weakened that they were forced to abandon their campaign and withdraw to Wilmington, North Carolina, for refitting.

Ensign of Soissonnois Regiment

A Hussar

A Naval Officer

A Grenadier

Count Rochambeau

The French in America. In July 1780, a French army of 6000 men under General Rochambeau landed in America. There were white-uniformed infantrymen from veteran regiments, artillerymen in blue uniforms, a colorfully outfitted unit of hussars, Royal marines and some black colonial units from the French West Indies. The French alliance, with the military and naval forces it provided, now gave a preponderance to the American cause.

The Battle of the Chesapeake Capes. The French Admiral de Grasse fought a severe but indecisive battle with the British fleet off Cape Henry on September 5, 1781. He was joined by a squadron of reinforcements under Admiral de Barras a few days later and the outnumbered

British were forced to retreat to New York. By establishing control over Chesapeake Bay, the French made the defeat of Cornwallis a certainty.

The French at Yorktown. In October 1781, George Washington and his French allies had the British army, under Lord Cornwallis, trapped at Yorktown, Virginia. Outnumbered by more than three to one, the British were gradually driven back, their positions taken, one by one, by the combined French and American assaults. French siege guns pounded the surviving British positions, and the French fleet's control of Chesapeake Bay made relief by the British fleet impossible.

The Surrender at Yorktown. Cornwallis requested a temporary truce, but Washington demanded an immediate surrender. The British commander capitulated on October 19, 1781. Humiliated, Cornwallis sent an adjutant to surrender his sword. Washington, always sensitive to protocol, refused to accept it himself, but ordered one of his staff to receive it. The British garrison marched out, with drums beating, to lay down their arms. Yorktown was the last significant battle of the war.

The Treaty of Paris. Through 1782 peace negotiations were labored over in Paris. The formal peace treaty between Great Britain and the new United States of America, signed on September 3, 1783, recognized the complete independence of the 13 former colonies. The American representatives at Paris were (left to right): John Jay, John Adams, Benjamin Franklin and Franklin's grandson, William Temple Franklin, secretary to the American delegation.

Washington's Farewell. On December 4, 1783, at a dinner at Fraunces Tavern in New York City, Washington took formal leave of his officers. He then traveled on to Annapolis, where he resigned his commission on December 23 and returned to his beloved estate at Mount Vernon, Virginia, to resume farming. Washington was called on to act as President of the Constitutional Convention of 1787 and to serve as the first President (1789–97) of the nation he had done so much to found.

45